PRISONERS OF BRIMSTONE PASS

A Clay Jared Western

R. Annan

Prisoners of Brimstone Pass
Copyright 2015 by R. Annan
E. 1.1
WGA Reg. #: R31618 (10/20/15)

Photography © L. Annan
Editor: Karren Doll Tolliver

One Vision Publishing
ISBN: 978-1-942338-42-0 (eBook)
ISBN: 978-1-942338-41-3 (Print)

Other Western books by R. Annan:

Fight for the Lazy M
The Gunfighter in Winter
Long Ride to Hell's Kitchen
Owl Hawks
Gunfight at Barfield Springs
Shootout at Sanctuary City
Last Days of a Gunfighter
Red Bandana
Copperhead Moon
Cowboys of the Box R

Dedication

To All My Readers

1.

When Clay Jared rode into Belcher Springs on a Friday afternoon in February looking for a job, he went to the Blue Duck Saloon. Speaking to a bartender was a good way of finding out who was who and what was what. It was like having a private tutor deliver a seminar on the local establishments.

It was still early in the afternoon and the Blue Duck wasn't crowded. There were a dozen cowboys at most. Five were at a poker table, four were at the bar and three were standing by the window talking.

Jared ordered a local beer called Momma's Milk and bought two boiled eggs. He ate the eggs slowly and took sips of Momma's Milk between bites. He found the drink flat and sour. So much for Momma's Milk. Jared chased it down with a shot of homemade rotgut, which wasn't any better.

After staring at Jared from the corner of his eye, the bartender finally approached him.

"Where you from, stranger?"

"Came up from a place near Haverston Junction."

"Haverston Junction? Didn't a place down there jest have a range war? Seems I heard they did."

"Oh? What did you hear?"

"I heard a big rancher tried ta ride roughshod over a smaller one an' got his ass kicked good." The bartender chuckled. "Real good."

"Yeah. Something like that."

"You lookin' fer a job?"

"Yep."

"What's yer specialty, friend?"

"Mostly cow poking."

"Well, there's three places a-takin' on new hands fer the spring roundup," the bartender said. "The Flyin' B, the Lazy T an' the Diamond G."

Jared mused a bit over that information then asked, "If you were me, which one would you pick?"

"Me? The Flyin' B, I reckon."

"Which pays the most?"

"The Diamond G, but you don't want ta go there, friend."

"Why not?"

The bartender stared over at the far table where the five men were playing poker.

"Ya see thet young buck a-wearin' those fancy clothes and thet pearl-handled Colt?"

Jared took a quick look.

"Yeah. What about him?"

"He's the son of the owner of the Diamond G, Jim Gadden. He's one wild brat. He messes with all the cowboys out there and is real mean around horses. Treats 'em like dirt."

"Oh?"

"Yeah. I'm jest a-sayin'. You probably wouldn't like it out there. Nobody does."

"Is that why they pay the most?" Jared chuckled.

"Yep. An' thet's why they're always a-hirin'." The bartender poured Jared another rotgut. "An' another thing. The kid likes ta brace the hired hands inta a gunfight."

"No kidding!"

"Nope. He's winged a couple real bad. I kid you not!"

"Killed any?"

"Not as yet. But someday he jest might. They don't shoot back ta hurt him, bein' the boss's son an' all."

Jared nodded and took another quick glance back at the table. He got caught. Two men dressed in black stared back at him for a moment then went on playing cards.

"Who is he with?"

"That's Bix Rawls and Kent Danton. Ya don't want ta mess with them, friend. They're trouble."

"I think I already have," Jared chuckled.

The back table erupted into a shouting match.

"Uh-oh! Here it comes," the bartender said painfully. "Ya better git ready ta duck!"

Jared turned in time to see one of the cowboys jump up and yell, "Danton, you cheatin' bastard!"

He didn't get very far. Two shots came from under the table and hit him dead center in the chest. He flipped backwards over his chair onto the floor and lay still.

"Damn it!" the bartender groaned.

Everyone in the Blue Duck stared back at the table. A cowboy at the bar quickly left, nodding at the bartender.

"He's a-goin' fer the marshal," The bartender said. "This should be fun."

Moments later an old man with sideburns and long, silver hair hanging down under his big brown Stetson ambled slowly in through the batwing doors. He waited until his eyes adjusted to the poor light and made his way back to the body, pulling nervously on his bushy mustache.

"Who drilled him?" the marshal asked in a rusty voice.

No one answered.

"I said, who the hell shot him?"

"He shot himself, Marshal Sawtrell," the young man said, chuckling. Rawls and Danton laughed.

The marshal stared down at young Gadden.

"Curt, yer keepin' wild company these days, aincha?"

Curt Gadden smiled smugly.

"Yer Dad wouldn't like ya hangin' out with these two varmints, would he now?"

"To hell with my dad, Marshal," Curt said with a sneer.

Bix Rawls and Kent Danton stood up and stretched as if bored. They were both big men with rugged faces. Rawls had a knife scar along his left cheek near his eye. Danton was ugly as sin, with a huge nose and a wart on his neck.

"Who tha hell you callin' a varmint, Marshal?" Rawls growled. "You'd better swallow thet, ya ol' fart!"

The bartender grabbed a scattergun from under the bar and pointed it down at Rawls.

"Thet's about enough fer one day, boys," he growled.

Rawls and Danton raised their hands.

"Sure, Fred, whatever ya say, my friend," Rawls said. "We were jest a-leavin', wasn't we, Kent ol' buddy?"

Kent Danton nodded.

The two gunmen started to pick up their winnings and leave.

"Not so fast, Rawls," the marshal said. "I'll have six double eagles fer the burial."

"Hell, his horse, saddle an' bags will pay fer thet."

"Nevertheless, I'll still take six!"

"Here, you crooked ol' fart!" Rawls hissed and tossed the eagles on the table.

He and Danton walked slowly towards the batwing doors, staring at Jared as they went by. The cowboy turned his back to them as they passed, watching their reflection in the mirror behind the bar. He slowly dropped his right hand down by his Colt. They, too, glanced into the mirror to get a good look at Jared's face as they left.

Young Curt Gadden came up to the bar, grabbed a boiled egg from the brine jar and stuffed it into his mouth.

"Give me a whiskey, Fred," he demanded.

"Go home, Curt," Fred said, putting the scattergun away.

"Come on, Fred! Just one!"

"It's suppertime, kid. Go home."

"Screw you, Fred!"

The boy stomped outside. The marshal came up to the bar.

"I'll go get the buckboard, Fred," the old man said. "Don't let nobody steal the body."

Fred chuckled. "Sure thing, Marshal."

The marshal left and returned a half hour later with the buckboard, complaining that the town council were too tight to hire a deputy. Fred the bartender and Jared carried the body out and loaded it. Then the lawman drove away to the undertaker's place.

Jared had noticed that the dead cowboy was young, probably in his mid-twenties.

"Who was he?" he asked.

"A cowboy from the Box J," the bartender answered. "The marshal will notify them in the morning."

Jared finished his drink, plunked down a double eagle and rode across town to the stockyard. The depot office was located next to the Cattlemen's Association building. Jared went in and stood before the chip-board and looked for the Diamond G. There were four chips with a G stamped on both sides hanging on a nail on the board under the Diamond G's name. Jared took one and left.

It was too late to ride out there so the cowboy walked his horse over to the stables a few yards away from the depot. He rented a stall for the night and got a feedbag of oats for his horse. He stripped off the riding gear and brushed the animal down as it ate, then led it to the trough to drink.

It was dark by then and both Jared and his horse were tired. He made his bed in one corner of the stall, laying out his bedroll. Using his saddle for a pillow he lay there wondering why he had chosen the Diamond G over the others.

He fell asleep without coming up with a satisfactory answer.

2.

John Gadden's Diamond G ranch was over 600,000 acres big. He had over 300,000 head of cattle. He was also a widower with a pair of headstrong twins, Curt and Sherry, both nineteen. The ranch and the cattle were easier to manage than the twins. Curt was wild and unmanageable, and Sherry was just plain spoiled. She knew how to get her way. As hard as he tried, Jim Gadden just couldn't bring himself to refuse his daughter anything.

Sherry Gadden was the spitting image of her mother. Tall and slim, she had short, corn-yellow hair, blue eyes, a small, straight nose and a seagull-wing shaped, pouting mouth that drove every rancher's son in the area crazy. And it was her pleasure do so, keeping them all at arm's length.

Her father had tried to marry her off several times, but, to his everlasting frustration, she rejected every one of his choices. There were more broken hearts in the valley than there were cattle. Young, beautiful Sherry Gadden was one wild thing no one had yet been able to tame. And it looked like no one ever would.

Gadden had sent both Curt and Sherry east for a formal education, but that didn't work out too well for Curt. He got tossed out and sent home time and time again. Finally, his father gave up and let him have his head like an unbroken mustang.

What with running the ranch, Jim Gadden was too busy to clamp down on the young boy. But he also feared he would someday regret not doing so.

As for young Curt Gadden, he was totally obsessed with practicing his fast draw by shooting at bottles and cans, gambling and hanging out with the riff-raff at the Blue Duck Saloon in Belcher Springs. He couldn't care less about ranching and even refused to get in on the roundups and branding. He treated both cattle and horses with complete contempt and often left his mounts with spur cuts on their groins.

The boy was especially hard on horses and enjoyed the act of breaking one in. Crushing the animal's spirit and will seemed to give him pleasure. Once, while in the process of taming a maverick, he was thrown to the ground four times. After being thrown the fifth time he got up and shot the horse in the head. After that the Diamond G cowhands stayed out of his way. They wanted nothing to do with him.

As for the women in Belcher Springs, they loved the boy for his free-spending ways. He would toss money around like water, especially when he had had too much to drink. Then he would order round after round of drinks and bought kisses for ten dollars a smack.

"Put it on my dad's tab!" were the boy's favorite words.

Two of Curt Gadden's friends were Bix Rawls and Kent Danton, both men of uncertain occupations. It was obvious they were not cowboys. They came and went like the wind but usually ended up at the Blue Duck Saloon playing poker on Fridays. Both men were good at cards but sometimes they were called out for cheating. This usually ended in a shootout with some cowboy lying dead beside the poker table. Rawls and Danton were very fast on the draw, and Curt Gadden idolized them both.

The boy looked forward to meeting them every Friday night at the Blue Duck. He often lost large sums of money to them but didn't seem to care. What he wanted most was to be accepted into their little circle. He wanted their blessing almost in a religious way.

So far they'd taken the kid's money but kept him at arm's length because they didn't want any trouble with his father.

What ate most at the boy's father was the fact that his only male heir had no interest in the Diamond G ranch.

As for Sherry Gadden, her father spent more time with her than he did with Curt. She had learned to ride and shoot under his guidance and could do both as well as any cowboy. To prove she could, she had put away her dresses at a young age and took up wearing cowboy clothes. From head to toe she was a cowgirl and could rope a steer and brand a calf with the best of them. She was also good at fixing up cuts, bruises and sprains suffered by the ranch hands. Some jokingly referred to her as Doc Sherry.

But Sherry Gadden was also as headstrong as her twin brother. She refused to go back East and get a higher degree. Nor would she consider marrying her father's handpicked choices.

"I'll pick my own man, Dad," she said time after time.

"You're nineteen, girl," Gadden would say, "best get serious about it before ya turn into an old maid!"

Sherry would smile, kiss her father on the cheek and say, "Dad, when I meet the man I want, I'll take him. So don't you fret none about that."

"You kin have any rancher's son in the valley. Just pick one and he's yours."

"Sure I can, Dad. I know that."

Jim Gadden would always give up the fight and take a walk in the yard, thinking about the future of his two children. He was worried that he couldn't save Curt and Sherry from themselves or others.

There were many evils in the world and some of them lived in Belcher Springs and the valley as well.

3.

Clay Jared got up early. He stretched, spoke to his horse, left the stable stall and walked over to the Belcher Springs beanery where he had a slow breakfast of ham, eggs, grits and coffee. It had been a cold February night and there was a dusting of snow on the ground, but the sun was climbing a clear sky so it looked like it would warm up a bit.

He returned to the stable, saddled up his horse and rode out for the Diamond G ranch, following the directions given by the stable owner.

It was midday when he passed through the front gate into the yard. He stopped to take a quick survey. There was nothing new or out of place. A big, two-story, whitewashed, clapboard house sat to the left. To the rear of it were the barn and corral. To the right of that was the windmill. Further right but up front was the squat, rectangular bunkhouse with its outside washstand and hitching rail. A slanted-roof shed was attached to the right side of the bunkhouse. A chuck wagon there faced into the shed. Under the shed were three long, eating benches.

An old, back-bent cook worked over a huge steaming pot on a fired-up range stove in front of the chuck wagon. Jared could smell the stew. He chuckled. Everything was as it should be. Stray chickens, cats, dogs and even a few ducks ran about the open area between the barn and the corral.

The smell of the onions and turnips drew him up to the shed. He dismounted, leaving his horse out in the yard as he sauntered under the shed and over to the chuck wagon. The cook saw him and turned to meet him.

"Son-of-a-gun stew?" Jared asked.

The old man laughed. "It must be okay ifn ya kin call it by the smell." The old man stroked his stubbly chin.

He wasn't much to look at, just an old has-been cowboy who couldn't wrangle anymore. He'd seen his day and paid his dues and now the only thing left for him to wrangle was a chuck wagon. It was his last stand before the grave.

"It does smell good," Jared said.

The old man had a white towel wrapped around his neck to keep out the February cold. He tightened it up.

"You lookin' fer tha rammy?"

"The ramrod? Yes." Jared answered.

"He should be back any minute now. He's out at the east graze," the cook said. Jared nodded.

Suddenly, loud voices came from the house. It sounded like an argument. Two male voices and one female clashed. There were shouts and threats.

"Uh-oh! Better run! They're at it agin!" the old man said, snickering.

"Who?" Jared asked.

"All of 'em. Mr. Gadden. The boy. The girl."

"What's the fight about?"

"Seems as the boss has hidden the kid's saddle so he can't ride inta town. He's done it before."

"Who's the woman? His wife?"

"Naw, he's a widower. Thet's Sherry, his daughter."

Suddenly Curt Gadden rushed out onto the porch and stopped to look around.

"You better grab yer horse, mister!" the cook said.

"What?"

Before the old man could reply, Curt Gadden cleared the porch in one leap. He ran over to Jared's horse, grabbed the reins and sprang into the saddle.

Jerking the horse's head sideways, the boy jammed his spurs into its barrel. The startled animal bawled in pain and twisted around, trying to take a bite out of the boy's left leg. It couldn't quite reach the target and ended up whirling around like a dog chasing its tail.

Jared rushed over and caught the horse's bridle in one hand, the left stirrup in his right and flipped the boy over the side. He hit the ground with a thud and scrambled backwards to avoid the animal's thrashing hooves.

Under Jared's familiar touch, the horse settled down.

Curt Gadden jumped up, dusted himself off and then glared with rage at Jared.

He immediately took up the gunman's stance.

"Draw, you son of a bitch!" the boy yelled.

Jared ignored him. He walked his horse over to the hitching rail by the bunkhouse and tied the reins.

"I said draw, you bastard!"

Jared stepped out into the yard, facing the boy.

"You've got a foul mouth, kid."

"Draw you piece of crap or I'll drill you where you stand."

Jared walked slowly straight at Curt Gadden, staring at him. A look of surprise swept over the boy's face.

"I saw you in town, at the saloon," the boy growled. "What the hell you doing out here?"

"I came to spank your ass, kid," Jared growled as he closed the distance.

"Don't come any closer, you son of a bitch! I'll kill you!"

Jared was three feet away when the kid drew. The cowboy swung a roundhouse right that knocked the boy to his knees. He fired his gun into the ground and fell back, unconscious. Jared stood over him, staring down, wondering what he should do next. He looked over at the old cook who seemed to be enjoying Jared's awkward situation.

Suddenly someone was behind Jared pounding him on the back, flailing away with their fists. Jared turned and backed away so he could get a look at his attacker.

For a moment he was stunned.

All Jared knew was that a beautiful young girl, almost a woman, was taking the fight to him for all she was worth. She got in a few good strikes before he was able to grab her wrists and pull her close. Her big blue eyes glared hatefully up at him.

"Sherry! Stop that!"

Jared glanced over towards the house. A tall, lean man was walking toward him. He was distinguished looking and had streaks of silver in his hair. Jared knew he was the owner of the Diamond G.

Sherry Gadden stopped struggling. She pulled away from the cowboy but her eyes never left him.

"Did you see what this saddle bum did to Curt, Dad?"

Jim Gadden picked up his son's gun then watched him struggle to sit up. He turned to Jared with half a smile on his lips.

"Yes, I did," Sherry's father said. It almost sounded as if he was pleased.

"Well, what are you going to do about it, Dad?"

Gadden stroked his chin, thinking. He looked at Jared and smiled.

"What's your name, cowboy?" he asked.

"Jared. Clay Jared, sir."

Just then a lone horseman rode into the yard and dismounted. He came over and stared down at the boy who was rubbing his jaw.

"What happened ta Curt, Mr. Gadden?"

Sherry Gadden burst out, "This man attacked Curt, Phil!"

"Why?" Phil, the big-shouldered ramrod, was smiling at Jared as if to say good work.

The old cook cut in with, "Because the kid tried ta steal his horse is why."

"Is thet so?" Phil asked Jared.

"Let's say the kid tried to borrow it without asking first."

Curt stood up on wobbly legs. Sherry came over to support him.

"Are you okay, Curt?" she asked. Her brother shoved her away.

"Give me my gun, Dad! I'm going to kill that bastard."

"Go into the house and clean up," Jim Gadden growled.

Suddenly the boy grabbed the gun from his father's hand and pointed it at Jared. The old cook jumped in front of the cowboy to protect him.

"You wanna shoot ol' Tim, sonny?" he chuckled. "Well, go right ahead an' shoot me, boy."

Curt Gadden seemed to shrink in on himself. He holstered his pearl-handled Colt and shrugged.

"No, I wouldn't shoot you, Tim," the boy said. He turned and went into the house.

The rancher looked over at Clay Jared.

"Well, Mr. Jared, what can I do for you?"

Jared pulled the Diamond G chip out of his coat pocket and held it up.

"You came for a job?" Gadden asked, as if insulted.

"Yes, sir."

"You come here and knock my son senseless and you want me to hire you?" Gadden turned to his ramrod. "What do you think, Mr. Newly? Do you think I should hire this man?"

"Hire him, Dad!"

"What?" Gadden looked at his daughter in disbelief. "Did you say to hire him, baby?"

"Yes."

"Why?"

"So I can make his life miserable for what he did to Curt. I'll make him wish he was dead!"

Gadden looked at his ramrod. "It's your call, Mr. Newly. Do you want a man like this working under you?"

The ramrod stared at Jared a moment then nodded.

"Yep, I do. An' we better grab him before he goes over ta the Box J or the Circle L, sir."

Jim Gadden shook his head in confusion.

"Welcome to the Diamond G, Mr. Jared," the rancher said. "I don't envy you having made an enemy of my daughter. She can be very difficult. You'd best stay out of her way."

"Oh, I intend to, sir."

Sherry Gadden gave Jared a curious look and followed her father back to the house.

She had a smile on her pretty lips.

4.

Bix Rawls and Kent Danton robbed banks, trains, houses and businesses and even rustled cattle whenever the opportunity presented itself. On many an occasion they had even rustled some Diamond G cattle, too.

They operated on a small scale, always wore a disguise and dressed like cowboys. While in Belcher Springs, however, they wore their black gunslinger outfits to impress the local gentry and the women. The girls at the Blue Duck were quite taken by them, especially as they were free spenders and big tippers.

One day they caught the eye of a young rich boy named Curt Gadden. To him, they were the real West, the West of the gunfighter and the fast draw.

At first Rawls and Danton were not amused by the kid and kept him at arm's length. They saw him for what he was, a headstrong, spoiled brat. However, when they found out that he was the son of the richest rancher in the area, they took a quick interest in him. They let him into their card games and made sure he lost. It wasn't long before they had a pile of IOUs with his name on them.

"When are we gonna go out to the Diamond G and cash those IOUs in, Rawls?" Danton asked one day.

"Not yet. Wait 'til he hits ten grand," Rawls said. "Then we'll ride out there and spring it on the old man."

"Wow! Ten grand! Christ, this kid's better than robbin' banks," Danton said.

"Yeah, he sure is. An' he's as stupid as the day is long."

One day they saw Sherry Gadden coming out of Carver's Mercantile with an armful of packages.

They stopped a lady who was walking in their direction.

"Excuse me, ma'am," Danton said, removing his hat in respect. "Kin you tell me who that lovely woman is?"

The woman glanced across the street. "Why, yes, that's Jim Gadden's daughter, Sherry Gadden."

"Oh? Is she any kin of young Curt Gadden?"

"She's his sister," the woman replied and walked on.

Danton chuckled. "My, oh, my! She is somethin', ain't she, Rawls?"

"Yeah," Rawls replied smiling. "She surely is."

Danton watched as the young woman drove away in a buckboard.

"I wonder how much her daddy would pay fer her?"

"Quite a lot, I'd reckon," Rawls mused.

"You think twenty grand?"

"Sure," Rawls said, "but it would be risky."

"Hell, she'd be worth it."

"Yer askin' fer trouble, pard," Rawls warned. "They'd come after us right quick with hangin' ropes a-danglin'."

"Yeah, but by then we'd be on our way with thet twenty grand all the way ta Mexico!" Danton said boldly. "We could buy us a hacienda and have all the senoritas an' tequila we want."

Rawls decided to humor his friend.

"I'll drink to thet, Kent," he said while thinking kidnapping a woman was a step too far, even for him.

5.

The day after Jared signed on at the Diamond G, the ramrod, Phil Newly, took him aside.

"I'm takin' ya out to the line shacks, Jared. You'll have ta know where they are because you'll be spendin' a lot of time out there pullin' in strays." Jared nodded. "An' take notice as we ride out. If it snows agin like it did last month, they'll be hard ta find."

"Sure," Jared said.

That Saturday the two of them rode out.

"There's three line shacks," the ramrod explained. "West, north and east. We'll head west first, then north and east."

The ground beneath them was rock-solid frozen by the February weather. The horses' metal shoes rang out as they rode at a brisk pace, their heads down against the biting of the wind. They crossed fields of dry prairie grass and short blue gamma and soon passed cattle huddling in bunches against the cold.

Further on they saw cattle bunched around hay feeds that were being dropped off by the haying crews, and further on still Jared saw the pickup cowboys bringing cattle in from the outlands.

They hit the west line shack the evening of the first day. A cowboy there named Thompson had shot a wild turkey and was roasting it over an open hearth that had an iron grate. He invited them in to eat.

The shack was well stocked with eating utensils and cookware. It also had a small larder with a tin of lard and plenty of seasonings for cooking. It had two bunks, a pile of firewood and a stream ran close by.

They stayed there overnight and on Sunday morning headed north to the furthermost reaches of the Diamond G.

They reached the remote north line shack just before dark. They ate supper, stayed for the night and, on Monday after breakfast, rode on again for the east line shack. Once more they stayed overnight. Tuesday evening found them riding into the yard of the Diamond G.

They were saddle-sore and tired.

"It's a big spread," Jared admitted.

"Sure is. You think you kin find them line shacks, Jared?" Newly asked.

"Sure, boss," Jared answered.

"Good, then."

They walked their tired horses down to the barn for a feed and a brushing. After that Newly went into the bunkhouse and Jared sat around by the range stove with the old cook, drinking hot coffee.

Finally, he began to nod off. He went into the bunkhouse to sleep.

About a week later, a late February storm hit the Belcher Springs area. It snowed for three days. In the morning wolf tracks could be seen in the alleyways and on the town's main street. Cats and dogs went missing.

Ramrod Phil Newly called Jared into his room.

"I'm sending you up to the west line shack to relieve Thompson, Jared. Take two extra blankets. One fer you and one fer yer horse. Take extra oats fer it, too. It'll be cold up there. Make sure ya got plenty of bullets. You'll need 'em."

"Wolves?"

The ramrod nodded.

"Bigger. Mountain cats, too. They'll take a man down as well as a calf. So be careful."

"How long?"

"Two weeks at least. Maybe three. Bring all the strays down to the mid-way pickup point. You okay with thet?"

"Sure," Jared said. He knew he had no choice. Newly was just being polite.

The next morning after breakfast, Jared went down to the barn to see the carpenter. He was in charge of signing out the extra gear and food. He knew the routine and began packing Jared's saddlebag.

"There's a can of whistle berries, love apples and music roots. Some Arbuckles, too. Jerky, hardtack and a can a peaches."

Jared got extra bullets for his Winchester and Colt, then rode out for the west line shack.

It was clear going until late afternoon when it started to snow again. That made it seem like a very long ride. Sometimes the wind blew so hard he had to grab the saddle horn to stay upright. He soon could hear wolves announcing his presence.

Thompson was glad to see him. That night they sat around the fire listening to the howling of the wind mixing with the howling of the wolves. The line shack shook on its foundation.

"You'll see their tracks," Thompson said. "They sometimes come right up to the door and scratch on it at night." He seemed spooked. "They know yer in here."

Jared sipped his coffee but didn't say anything.

"There's this big lobo," Thompson went on. "He's the alpha. Big guy. Probably weighs one-fifty or two hundred."

"That's pretty big," Jared said, as if he had his doubts.

"Yeah, too damn big if ya ask me. He tracked me once. I took a shot but missed him. He's fast as lightnin'."

In the morning after Thompson left, Jared noticed wolf tracks all around the line shack.

6.

A day after Thompson left it began to snow again. Jared didn't go out until it stopped on the second day. By then the snow was deep, and that was dangerous. The horse could step on a rock and twist its ankle or step in a hole and break a leg.

He rode slowly along looking for strays but didn't find any. The snow and cold had driven many down toward the pickup point miles below.

As he came up to a rise he heard the bawling of a cow on the other side. In a few minutes he saw why. A pack of wolves were feasting on a calf. The mother stood yards away bawling.

The alpha wolf saw Jared and came out in front to do battle. Jared slowly pulled his Winchester from its sheath and dismounted. He walked a few feet forward and stopped to stare. He was fascinated. What a beautiful, powerful looking beast it was.

The alpha warned him off with a deep, throaty, snarling growl, its yellow fangs dripping blood.

As Jared took a step backward it hunched down in an attack position, glaring at the cowboy with blazing green eyes.

Suddenly the horse whinnied and snorted, stomping the ground. Jared spun around to see it kick out at two wolves attacking from the side. The horse's steel-clad rear hooves caught one in the ribs, sending it rolling and howling. The second wolf went for the animal's rear legs, trying to cripple it and bring it down.

Jared dropped the Winchester in the snow, drew his Colt and fanned off a shot. The bullet caught the wolf in mid-air, dropping it at the horse's feet. The frightened animal bolted and ran off down the rise.

The hairs on the back of Jared's neck tingled as he swung around. The alpha hit him square in the chest. It felt like a blow from a sledgehammer, and the cowboy went flat on his back in the snow, dropping his Colt on the way.

The alpha landed on all fours a few yards away and whirled about to face Jared. For a moment neither man nor beast moved. The animal crouched forward in the springing position and hunched its neck to glare hatefully up at its enemy.

Jared could feel the intense power of that hate and suddenly he realized his hand was shaking, not from the cold but from pure fear for his life.

Moving ever so slowly, Jared retreated, feeling in the snow for his Colt as he moved. The alpha came at him with a snarl, its blood-stained teeth glistening in the sunlight. The wolf's body lifted effortlessly into the air, arched over and closed the gap between them in one leap.

Jared raised his left arm high to ward off the attack. The alpha caught it just above the wrist, bit down and pulled the cowboy down on his side, dragging him along by his arm.

The other wolves were beginning to take notice when Jared felt the Winchester under his free hand where he had dropped it in the snow. He grabbed it by its stock, brought it up and then down on the beast's snout. It howled in pain and backed off a few feet, staring at Jared in surprise. The cowboy pointed the rifle at it. It crouched down to protect its belly and moved slowly backwards.

Jared fired a shot over its head and it spun around and ran off. The rest of the pack followed. He fired over their heads again to keep them moving. Moments later they were out of sight around a hill.

Jared looked around in a daze. The cow had run off and his horse was nowhere in sight. He stood up and inspected his arm. His wool mackinaw had blunted the alpha's bite somewhat, but the fangs had gone into the flesh and his arm was bleeding.

He shook his head to clear it and looked around for his Colt. He finally found it, stuck it back in his holster and started to walk away. As he passed the two wolves, the one his horse had kicked looked up at him and snarled. He shot it in the head with the Winchester and kept moving.

He was about five miles from the cabin when it began to snow again, heavier this time. He hurried on, trying to follow the horse's tracks before they disappeared. About an hour later he saw a red spot in the distance. It was the color of the shack.

Half frozen and exhausted, he stumbled into the line shack just as dark was falling. He collapsed on the bunk, burning with fever. He could hear the wolves howling in the woods close by and knew they were coming to get him. After a while he thought he heard them sniffing at the door.

His arm felt hot and swollen where it was bitten. It throbbed and pulsed as if alive. He started to feel cold and thought about making a fire but put it off for the moment.

Struggling out of his coat, Jared looked at the wound. It was already showing signs of being infected. He got a bottle of whiskey from the saddlebag, poured it over the punctured, raw flesh and gasped in pain, almost passing out. Finally, he got a cotton bandage from the medicine box and wrapped it around the throbbing wound.

Jared moved slowly, getting wood from the wood box to start a fire in the hearth. When he got it going he sat close to it to get warm. At first he felt nothing so he threw more wood into the flames, building them up until he could feel the heat. It made him nod off. Once he almost fell into the fire, so he crawled into his bunk, wrapped himself in two blankets and fell into a nightmarish sleep.

When he awoke it was daylight.

Although he felt weak he remade the fire then took the Winchester and a pail out to the stream behind the line shack. Breaking through the ice, he filled the pail and returned to make coffee. He tried to eat but couldn't. Even the coffee tasted strange.

A quick look at the arm showed it was swollen. Pus was oozing from the teeth cuts. He poured whiskey on it again, screamed and almost fainted. Somehow he managed to crawl back to his bunk and lay down.

When Jared woke up again he had trouble focusing his eyes. It seemed as if the shack was full of an undulating, foggy mist. He tried to get up but couldn't. One moment he was sweating and the next he was shivering.

Suddenly he heard a noise outside. The door opened and something or someone came in. Jared strained to see what or who it was.

It was Sherry Gadden.

7.

Sherry Gadden held a hand against Jared's forehead. He was on fire.

"You have a bad fever. What happened?"

"I got bit by a wolf. What are you doing here?"

"I came to shoot you."

"Maybe you won't have to. I think the wolf killed me."

"I won't let you die."

"Why not?"

"Because I hate you."

She kissed him. Her lips felt cool and soothing on his parched mouth.

"I'm dreaming," he chuckled.

"No, you're not."

"Do that again."

She kissed him again.

"Let's look at the wound," Sherry said.

"Alright, Doc."

Jared fell back on the cot. Sherry looked at his arm.

"I'm going to do something to it," she said, "and it's going to hurt like hell."

"You're going to cut it off?"

"No, not that. Just lay back and think of something nice."

The girl went to the hearth and built a fire. She put the coffee pot on the flames until the water started to steam and bubble and then dropped a handful of coffee grounds into it.

"You're going to feel this. It's alright to faint."

Before he could answer she pulled his arm out and poured the hot coffee onto the wound. His scream echoed out into the woods. The wolves answered mockingly with a howl of their own.

The girl dumped the steaming coffee grounds on top of the bite, packing it firmly. Finally, she wrapped it tightly with a clean bandage. He stared at her through tear filled eyes.

"I'm not going to fight with you, Miss Gadden."

"We're not fighting."

She crawled under the covers next to him. He slept.

When he awoke it was daylight again and he wondered how long he had slept. Sherry was cooking over the grated hearth. The smell of ham, beans and coffee hung strong in the air.

"How long was I out?"

"Two days. You were a pain in the ass. You tried to take me."

"Did I?"

The girl giggled. "Not even close."

His arm felt much better. She had changed the dressing.

"I dreamed we were ---"

"That's all it was, just a dream." She turned her back to him.

"All of it?"

"Most of it."

"Which part was real?"

"I'm not saying."

They had breakfast. Later she got a pail of water from the stream and heated it on the fire.

"Can you wash?" she asked.

"Yes."

"Then you should do that."

Afterwards she dressed and put her coat on.

"Your horse is outside. I gave it some oats. I'm leaving now," she said. "It's not snowing."

"Thank you, Miss Gadden."

"For what?"

"Saving my life."

"Then you'll have to be my slave and do as I tell you."

"Alright. Tell me to do something."

"Kiss me goodbye."

She fell into his arms. When the kiss ended, she slapped him gently on the cheek and left.

After she was gone he realized what she had very skillfully done. He would have to leave the Diamond G. He had broken the code: Cowboys did not mess with an owner's daughter. Cowboys had a place and they stayed there. It was part of the code. Jared had crossed the line and he knew it.

If the word got out that she had come to Jared, her father would come at him with a vengeance. He chuckled. This was her way of getting revenge on him for hitting her brother. She had outfoxed him very easily and he helped her do it. The truth be told, he had no idea what he had done to her or if he had done anything. He had been delirious the whole time except when they'd kissed.

No matter. Her just spending three days with him at the line shack was enough to hang him if Jim Gadden wanted to.

The first thing the cowboy did after Sherry left was to check his horse. He hugged its neck, rubbed its ears, kissed it on the forehead and then examined every inch of its body. When he finished he let out a sigh of relief. The animal was fine.

For two days he stayed close to the line shack, watching for the alpha wolf and his pack. On the third day he rode out to where the fight had been and saw crows eating the remains of the calf. When they saw him they scattered up into the birches. Wolf tracks led north. Jared followed them for a mile then came back to the shack to get warm.

The next day Jared rode out to look for strays. He found over five hundred in a small, sheltered valley ten miles east of his location and drove them south into another area where he found about two hundred more. He slept out in a stand of aspen, keeping a fire going the whole night. In the morning he rode out again. This time he brought back over six hundred.

He bunched them together and got them heading south. After a few miles a leader emerged and that made it easy to keep them tight. Jared's horse was having a good time. Like any trained quarter horse, it was fast and could stop quickly and turn in a small circle. Without his horse Jared would never have gotten the herd down to the south pick-up point where two cowboys latched onto it and shuttled it down to the branding area.

He rode back to the line shack, three days away. When he got there he was exhausted.

8.

The best thing that could be said about Bix Rawls and Kent Danton was that they were lazy. The backbreaking, teeth-jarring work of a cowboy was not for them. They had tried it once and that was more than enough to change their minds about riding for the brand.

In days gone by, they worked on a cattle ranch near the Pecos River just north of where it ran up to the Mexican border. The ranch was so large it had more cattle than it could keep count of. This made it easy for Rawls and Danton to cut out a few hundred and sell them over the border.

Rustling cattle became a habit with the two until one day they ran into a Texas Ranger ambush and barely escaped. That encounter with the law started them on their career of crime. They rode across the Devil River, up toward Sonora and on to San Angelo, robbing small banks along the way.

Drifting ever further north, they crossed the Brazos and continued into Oklahoma Territory, tossing in a few train robberies just for the fun of it.

Bix Rawls was good at cards so they used that as a front, passing themselves off as gamblers while robbing commuter trains and small town banks in the area but not too close to home. Since rustling was in their blood, however, when they saw a chance they took it. But everything they did was on a small scale.

And, as they were both fast with a gun, they wore the black of a gunslinger. It fitted them well and they milked that image for all it was worth.

By the time they rode into the cattle town of Belcher Springs, Kansas, they were tired of running. There wasn't much law there but plenty of drunken cowboys who liked to play poker. This suited Rawls and Danton just fine. They found a deserted line shack five miles from town and staked it out. It was perfect for their needs.

Early every Friday the two would ride into Belcher Springs, tie up at the Blue Duck Saloon, buy a bottle of rotgut, get several glasses and take a table. They never drank the whiskey. It was for the poor suckers who fell into their web. An open game of poker developed and they would keep the whiskey flowing.

"Is this an open game?"

"It sure is, cowboy! Sit down an' have a drink!"

By closing time they would walk out with a few hundred dollars in their pockets.

Rawls and Danton would usually sit across from one another so they could send their secret above the table signals by a wink, yawn, nod or a wiping of the nose. Under the table they had a one-two-three code of tapping each other's boot toes.

They nursed their drinks while they kept refilling the glasses of the other players. When the bottle was empty they got another. The cost was well worth the return.

Of the two, Rawls was the card sharp. He could plant an ace or a deuce in Danton's hand at will. He seldom planted one in his own hand and kept his winnings at a reasonable level so no one would get suspicious. He made it look like Danton was just plain lucky. Sometimes he let a cowboy win just to make sure the game looked to be on the level.

One Friday a young kid came into the Blue Duck and saw two black-clad gamblers playing cards at a table in the back. He was struck by their slick appearance and haughty manners. The kid was Curt Gadden and he had just had a fight with his father and was feeling his oats.

"Who are they?" the boy asked Fred the bartender.

"That's Bix Rawls and Kent Danton," Fred said. "Yer dad wouldn't want you messin' around with them two, Curt."

"To hell with my dad!"

The boy walked boldly over to the table and sat down with Rawls and Danton.

"I'm Curt Gadden," the boy boasted, reaching out to shake their hands. He pulled out a fistful of double eagles and laid them on the table. "Let's play poker."

Rawls and Danton had heard of Gadden's Diamond G because they had cut off a few of its cattle once. And here was the owner's son staring at them as if they were gods.

One day soon after, Rawls and Danton had a discussion about the boy.

"The kid's a pain in the ass, Kent," Danton said. "I'm sick of hearing about how much he hates his ol' man."

"Yeah, me too. But he's worth a few bucks at the table so don't do anything ta chase him away."

"How much does he owe us?"

"About three grand so far," Kent replied.

"Ya know, I was thinking we oughta squeeze the kid a little harder.

Rawls thought that over. "Not a bad idea. Get him ta sign some more paper."

That was when Curt Gadden started to lose heavily to Rawls and Danton. Rawls began to deal him lousy cards. In a few weeks they had him up to the desired amount of ten thousand dollars.

It was time to spring the trap on Jim Gadden.

9.

Sherry Gadden was worried about her brother. He was unusually sullen, brooded a lot and spent more time in Belcher Springs than he did at the Diamond G. And that bothered her.

One day, old Tim the cook cornered her.

"Miss Sherry?"

"What is it, Tim?"

"Kin we talk?"

"Of course, Tim. What is it?"

"It's about Curt, ma'am," Tim said holding his hat in his hands, fingering the brim nervously.

"What about him, Tim?"

"I didn't want to tell yer dad 'cause I know he'd explode on the boy. They fight enough as it is."

"Tell him what?"

"The boy's in deep trouble, Miss Sherry."

"How's that, Tim?"

"Wal, some of the boys have seen him consortin' with Bix Rawls an' Kent Danton at the poker table, ma'am. They've seen him a-signin' paper."

Sherry nodded. "I see. Well, you did the right thing by telling me and not my dad, Tim. I'll handle it."

This seemed to explain Curt's strange mood. He wasn't himself these days. He looked worried and now she knew why. He had gotten himself deep into debt and, if Jim Gadden found out about it, he would make life miserable for him.

But she would fix things up, just like she had taken care of that pest Clay Jared. The more she thought about it, the more she chuckled. It had been fun rattling his spurs. Now he was finished at the Diamond G. When he comes back in from the range, her dad would send him packing.

She was glad to be rid of him. Or was she? A voice inside her said she wasn't but she tried not to listen to it.

Sherry Gadden rode into Belcher Springs early in the afternoon wondering how she would handle the situation. By the time she tied her horse in front of the Blue Duck she decided to be bold. She would go on the attack.

She went boldly into the saloon, looked around and quickly saw the table where Curt sat with the two black-clad cowboys. From Tim's description she knew who they were. They saw her and stopped playing cards, staring at her as she came up to them. For a moment they looked surprised but quickly covered that with a smirk.

Her brother jumped up, a look of uncertainty on his face.

"Sis! Did Dad send you?"

"No one sent me, Curt, but you have to come home before he finds out." Her brother was unsteady on his feet and she could smell the whiskey on his breath.

"I'm finished at the ranch, Sis," Curt said in a thick voice. "Tell Dad to go to hell." He slurred his words.

Sherry grabbed her brother's arm and tried to turn him towards the door.

"It's his bid," Rawls said.

Sherry stopped and turned to stare at Rawls.

"Which one are you?"

"Bix Rawls, an' it's the kid's bid."

The young woman glared at Rawls.

"He's finished bidding and he's finished with both of you!" She turned back to Curt. He seemed sluggish and his eyes were half shut from drink. "Let's go home, Curt."

"He ain't goin' nowhere, lady," Danton said. "Not until somebody pays up."

"How much?"

"Ten thousand."

For a moment Sherry was stunned by the amount. She quickly recovered. "Alright, you'll get it."

"When?" Rawls asked.

Sherry searched her mind for a quick way out. "Today. Now. I'll go to the bank."

Danton chuckled. "You do that. But he stays here until you come back with the money, bitch."

Suddenly Curt pulled away from his sister and glared at Danton.

"Take that back, Danton!"

"Relax, kid," Danton said, smiling.

"You take that back! Now!" the boy yelled.

The Blue Duck Saloon went deadly quiet.

Danton grinned. "Sure. I'll take it back, kid. She ain't a bitch. She's a snobby bitch, jest like you, kid. Now set yer ass down an' make yer bid!"

"Draw!" Curt Gadden yelled as he pushed his sister away and went for his gun.

His bullet hit Danton low on the outside of his thigh. Rawls already had his gun out and fired once, hitting the boy in the chest. Then Danton shot him in the heart.

Sherry Gadden stood staring down at her dead brother's body as if in a trance, not believing what had just happened. She moaned painfully and knelt down by his side. His eyes stared up at her with a dull, blank look. All the light and life had gone out of them.

She screamed.

"Don't move, you two!"

Fred the bartender had his scattergun pointed at Rawls and Danton. "Go get the marshal, Ed!" A cowboy ran out through the batwing doors into the street yelling, "Murder!"

"Now, take it easy, Fred," Rawls said smoothly. "You saw what happened. The kid braced Danton. Everybody saw it."

"Yeah, an' you bushwhacked the kid! That's what I saw!"

Sherry stood up and flew at Danton, flailing away with her fists, screaming. He grabbed her and spun her around, using her as a shield.

"Go ahead and shoot, Fred!" he yelled.

"Let's git the hell outta here, Kent," Rawls yelled.

As Danton held the girl in front of him, Rawls pointed his gun at her head. They walked slowly toward the batwing doors.

"Drop thet scattergun, Fred, or I'll blow her brains out!" Rawls hissed. The bartender lowered his weapon.

Rawls and Danton inched their way slowly out onto the street to the horses and stopped. The marshal was waiting.

"Give it up, boys!" he hollered. He held his shotgun pointed at them. "You don't want ta do this!"

"Git the hell outta the way, Marshal!" Rawls said. "I'll kill her. I swear I will!"

"Now take it easy, Rawls!" The marshal backed off.

"There's a dead kid in there, Marshal!" Rawls yelled. "Ya best go get him buried or you'll be buryin' the girl, too!"

"Alright. Don't do nothin' rash, now."

"They shot Curt!" Sherry screamed. "Kill them!"

"Shut up, bitch," Danton growled, "Or yer next!"

"You can't git away with this, men," the marshal said. "You'll both hang!"

"Not where we're a-goin'," Danton chuckled.

Danton handed Sherry Gadden to Rawls, swung into his saddle and then hoisted her up onto the saddle swell while Rawls covered him. Rawls then leaped over the rump of his mount and they rode off down the street out of town.

Suddenly it started to snow hard. The marshal, Fred and several townsfolk stood on the street and watched helplessly as the killers and their prisoner disappeared into a wall of swirling white.

Sherry Gadden kicked and twisted to get free of Kent Danton. They were about five miles from Belcher Springs when she finally slipped out of his arms onto the ground.

Through the blanket of snow, she could just make out the town in the distance and ran in that direction.

"Leave her go, Kent," Rawls yelled, holding onto his hat. "We don't need her now!"

"The hell you say! She's worth plenty fer ransom!"

Danton nudged his horse and turned it around. Sherry was running as fast as she could against the wind. Several times she slipped on the snow and fell to her knees only to struggle up and start off again. He followed her, staying behind until she began to slow down and gasp for air.

Just as she was about to collapse he reached down and scooped her up behind the saddle horn.

"Behave, bitch, or I'll knock yer teeth out!" he growled in her ear. She went slack in his arms as he rode back to Rawls.

"We gotta move fast," Rawls yelled. "They'll be gettin' up a posse!"

"A lot of good it'll do 'em in this weather," Danton shouted back. "The snow's got us covered."

They rode close, almost touching.

"Where we headin'?" Danton asked.

"Brimstone Pass."

They put their heads to the wind and rode on.

10.

Jared was tired, cold and dirty. Twelve hours a day in the saddle was taking its toll. He had wrangled over two thousand strays down to the pick-up point. He hadn't shaved in over a week and had lost track of time. His pocket watch was his only reminder of civilization.

When he got back to the west line shack one evening a cowboy named Boggs was waiting.

"Christ, you stink, Jared."

"Kiss my ass, Boggs." Jared sat down on his bunk and took off his coat. "Whatta you doin' here?"

"They're callin' you in. I'm takin' over."

"How come?"

"Sherry Gadden's been stolen by Bix Rawls and Kent Danton."

"You're pulling my leg."

"Nope."

"Stolen, you say?"

"Yeah. An' they kilt the boy, too."

"Christ!"

"Yeah."

"And Gadden wants me back?"

"Yep."

"Why?"

"Hell, I don't know. Ask him when ya git there."

Jared left in the morning.

Two days later he rode into the yard of the Diamond G ranch. Jim Gadden rushed out to meet him. He looked older.

"I heard," Jared said. "Whatta you want me to do?"

"Get her back." Gadden's eyes were bloodshot from worry.

"Why me? Why not the law?"

"This is different. One of the cowhands told me what you did at the Box R. I'll make it worth your while."

It seemed Jared's reputation as a fast draw had caught up with him.

"Forget that. Where is she?"

"Brimstone Pass."

"Where the hell is that?"

"Tim knows. He'll go with you."

"Wouldn't a posse be best?"

"They won't go in there. It's an outlaw hideout. Like Hell's Kitchen."

Old Tim came out of the bunkhouse buttoning up his sheepskin mackinaw. He smiled at Jared.

"So, where is it, this Pass?" Jared asked.

"About fifty miles north of here," Tim said.

"Couldn't we at least take the marshal?"

"He ain't got no authority out there," Tim replied. "No lawman in his right mind would set foot in the Pass. He'd never git out."

"How do you know so much about the place?"

"I spent two years in Brimstone, Jared, an' when I came out the law got me and I did ten years in prison."

"What for?"

"A-robbin' an' a-rustlin'."

The old man cackled and scratched his whiskered jaw. For the first time Jared noticed the old man was a bit light in the head and that wasn't good. He might be better off going it alone.

"You were a bad boy, Tim," Jim Gadden said to the old man.

"I sure was, Mr. Gadden but I'm law abidin' now. Thet's fer sure. Thet's fer dang sure."

"Of course you are, Tim," the rancher said, patting the old timer on the shoulder. He winked at Jared.

Tim started to walk towards the corral.

"Where you going, Tim?"

"I'm gonna saddle up and go get Miss Sherry, Mr. Gadden."

"In the morning, Tim. And Jared will go with you."

The old man took his hat off, scratched his head in confusion and then put it back on.

"Oh, sure. In the morning."

He walked slowly back into the bunkhouse.

Jared gave Jim Gadden a questioning look.

"He'll be alright," the rancher said. "Once in a while he gets confused. He'll be fine."

"I hope so," Jared said. He sounded doubtful.

The rancher put a hand on Jared's shoulder. "Look, Jared, I don't have much to work with here. Somebody has to get her out of the Pass as quickly as possible. Bad things can happen to her there. Very bad things. Will you help?"

"You didn't have to ask, Mr. Gadden," Jared said. He paused a moment. "Maybe it's better I go alone, without the old man."

"I trust Tim with my life, Jared. He might seem a little crazy but he's not. You haven't seen him draw a gun. He's damn cool in a fight. And you won't get into the Pass without him."

Jared chuckled. "So, he's really in charge."

"Does that bother you?"

Jared shrugged. "No, I reckon not. He'll be worth a laugh, anyway."

"I'm sure he will," Gadden said.

Jared looked away for a moment to avoid Gadden's eyes.

"Did your daughter tell you she came out to the west line shack a few weeks ago?"

The rancher's eyes narrowed. Jared turned to face him.

"The hell you say!"

"Yes. I got bit by a wolf. She saved my life." Jared pulled the left sleeve of his coat and shirt above the wrist to expose the ugly scar. The rancher stared at it and nodded.

"Nothing else happened between you two?"

"No, nothing else happened."

"Thanks for telling me but you know what this means, don't you, Jared?"

Jared pulled his sleeve back down and nodded.

"Yes, sir, I know."

"And you're still going?"

"Yes."

"Thank you, then. You're a real cowboy, Jared."

Gadden walked away, his head down. Jared went into the bunkhouse.

11.

The place known as Brimstone Pass was a three-day ride north of Belcher Springs. It was the place where outlaws went when the hot breath of the law was breathing down their necks.

Around 1850, give or take a year, a polygamous religious sect discovered it and claimed it as their promised land. Over the years they built a thriving community and practiced their religion there undisturbed by the outside world.

It was well hidden and had only two ways in or out. One was on the south side through a pass in a wall of rocks that was covered by cottonwood and aspen. The other way out was on the north side. It led though a labyrinth of marshland and foul-smelling sulfur bogs. Wild mulberry trees, sumac, poison ivy vines and dense brush made it a very dangerous way to go.

On days when the north wind blew across the sulfur bogs it carried the strong smell of rotting eggs with it. The odor permeated the entire settlement. If you stayed in Brimstone Pass long enough, you hardly noticed it.

As the years went by, outlaws discovered the Pass. Some brought large amounts of money and were welcomed with open arms. Over time the demographics of Brimstone Pass changed. It came to be known as a good place to dodge the law. Outlaws came and went but many stayed and married since there were plenty of women to share in the polygamous social setup of that secluded place.

Religion eventually took a backseat to more worldly things such as drinking, gambling and gun fighting. It got so bad the outlaws themselves had to put a stop to the killing and taking of other men's women. A mayor was elected as a sort of referee to settle disputes in a civil manner. He was usually a person who was more educated than the others and could read and write. Eventually a primitive set of rules and regulations evolved and everyone was sworn to abide by them or leave the Pass.

By the early 1880s, Brimstone Pass had settled down to a stable status quo. It was a thriving outlaw community with a two-story hotel, a saloon and other small businesses. The church still stood but no one ever used it and it soon fell into disrepair. Anyone coming into Brimstone Pass with the idea of changing its morals met with bitter disappointment and utter failure.

Small time outlaws came into the Pass with the idea of enjoying their ill-gotten gains, spending it on women and gambling and then, when broke, sneaking out the north entrance and taking up robbing banks and trains again.

There was no way the law could control that exit with all its dense growth and smelly sulfur bogs. In some places the ground was as soft as quicksand. Quite a few outlaws never made their way out. Nature measured out its own form of justice as equally effective as a hangman's rope.

In many respects Brimstone Pass was a kind of hell. Fighting over women and cards usually ended in a burial. The life expectancy of an outlaw there was about five years. Alcoholism was rampant. Those who left by the front were usually seen by ranchers, farmers or other law-biding citizens. They soon were hunted down and hanged or sent to prison according to the seriousness of their crimes.

Brimstone Pass beckoned outlaws with open arms. Like a huge Venus flytrap, it ensnared its victims in a lure that would eventually snuff out their lives.

It was both a blessing and a curse, a sanctuary and a prison.

12.

Lester Notch, the mayor of Brimstone Pass, was not very happy.

"You can't bring no girl in here unless she's willin' to come here," he said. "An' she don't look like she's willin'."

"Relax, Mayor," Rawls replied. "Her an' Danton are gonna git hitched. She's his fee-on-say."

"Yeah, me and my little darlin' is a-gonna tie the knot an' settle here in the Pass. An you kin marry us."

"Well then, thet's different," the mayor conceded.

"We're gonna take a room down at the Pine Tree Hotel fer a while," Danton said. "Then we'll build us a place an' settle down. Her daddy is gonna send us some money ta start a little business here. Lots of money."

"He's lying!" Sherry Gadden yelled. She struggled to get away from Danton but her hands were tied and her feet were hobbled. "They shot my brother and the law is after both of them. My father will come in here and tear this filthy place apart!"

Danton laughed. "She's a wild one. She's jest playin' hard ta git. We're expectin' a baby soon."

"You lying son of a bitch!" Sherry screamed.

Danton clamped a hand over her mouth.

The mayor wasn't convinced on one side or the other. Most people who came into the pass were either crooked as the day is long, big liars, crazy, or a combination of all three. In any case, he couldn't do anything about it. The best thing to do was let it play out and see what would happen.

"Alright," Mayor Notch said. "Ya can stay so long as ya don't cause no trouble. Otherwise yer leavin'."

"Sure, sure, Mayor," Rawls said. He turned to Danton. "Let's go."

Rawls went out into the street with Danton forcing Sherry Gadden along. She could walk but the hobbles kept her from running, and with her wrists tied she couldn't fight back.

They walked down the street to the porch of a two story pine log building. There was a sign over the door that read: *Pine Tree Hotel and Yellow Dog Saloon. Welcome.* They stepped up on the porch and stopped.

"Listen," Rawls said to Sherry. "I'll untie ya if you promise not to run. If not ya kin stay tied day and night."

"Alright," Sherry said. "I promise."

"Just so ya know, there's no place ya kin hide here," Rawls added. "So don't try anything stupid."

He untied Sherry and put the ropes in his coat pocket. They went into the building.

The bottom floor was a saloon. On the right was a long, crude bar made of pine planks laid over several oak barrels. Two bartenders stood behind it serving half a dozen customers. Behind the bartenders was a counter lined with bottles of local brew. Each bottle had a handwritten label such as Skunk Stink, Possum Piss, Liquid Lava and so forth.

Behind the bottles was a large, flaking mirror that gave a weird, distorted image of people. When they were close they looked fat and when they were far away they looked skinny.

The room was well packed with local citizens of the Pass, both at the tables, the roulette wheel and the bar. It seemed unless you were a businessman there wasn't much to do in Brimstone except drink and gamble. Fighting over bargirls was also very popular.

Rawls and Danton took Sherry Gadden to a far table in the rear, out of the glare of the hanging oil lamps, so as not to attract undue attention. No one seemed to notice them.

As soon as they sat down, an elderly madam sauntered over to them. She was tall and had long, stringy, unkempt blonde hair that fell over her fleshy shoulders. In an attempt to look young and attractive she had overpainted her mouth and eyebrows to the point of being grotesque. Her pink dress was dirty and tattered, and large Spanish coins hung from her earlobes. A lot of cheap, bright, colored jewelry and beads adorned her body. She breathed heavily through a broken nose.

"I own the place. Lookin' fer a little action, gentlemen?" she said in a deep, rusty sounding voice. She stared at Sherry like a cat would at another cat intruding into its territory.

Rawls got up, took the madam aside and whispered to her. She glanced at Sherry and nodded. Rawls handed her several double eagles. The women tucked them into a pocket in her smoke-saturated dress and walked back to Sherry.

"Come with Lena, baby doll," she said in a raspy voice.

"I'm not going anywhere with you, lady," Sherry said.

Lena leaned over and slapped Sherry Gadden across the face, almost knocking her out of her chair. The girl gasped from the pain and held her hand to her face.

"Ya want another?"

"No."

"Then git the hell up!"

Sherry stood up slowly. The big woman grabbed her arm and pulled her over to the stairs leading to the second floor. Danton followed.

"Up!" Lena growled. The girl went up the stairs. Lena gave her a shove to get her moving faster.

They met men and women coming and going. At the top, the woman pointed down the hall and gave Sherry another shove. They went to the far end and stopped in front of a door with a sign that read: Madam Lena.

It was dark inside. Lena lit an oil lamp. When the light flared up Sherry saw a large brass bed and other furnishings. A single window looked out over the street.

"Sit, bitch!"

The madam shoved Sherry down on the bed and turned to Danton.

"Watch her a minute. I'll be right back."

She left and in ten minutes returned with two working girls. Danton gave them each a double eagle.

"Keep an eye on her. If she makes a move, belt her good," Danton told them. The painted ladies nodded.

Lena and Danton went back downstairs. The madam faced Rawls.

"I want more money."

"When the deal goes through, you'll git plenty."

"No, now, or she's outta here."

"Alright." Rawls reached into his pocket and took a fifty-dollar bank note from his billfold. "How's this?"

The woman inspected it. "For now, okay." She walked away.

Danton and Rawls sat down. Rawls didn't look very happy.

"What's the matter, Bix?"

"The girl. We shoulda left her like I said."

"It'll be fine."

"Don't ya see, ya asshole? We're trapped here! Jest like in jail! Prisoners! We can't even send word ta her daddy!"

"Whatta ya sayin'?"

"They ain't got no telegraph here, ya stupid bastard! How we gonna git a ransom?"

It suddenly dawned on Danton.

"Shit! We shoulda headed fer Mexico."

"Now ya say it! You fool! We coulda took her anyplace but here, but no, you said take her ta Brimstone! Damn you!"

They got a bottle of whiskey, drank it and rented a room for the night. In the morning they had breakfast at a local beanery and came back to the saloon to plan their next move.

"Why don't we put her ta work?" Danton suggested. "Make some money off her."

Rawls thought about that for a moment. "I don't know. She might kill herself before she'd let thet happen."

"Well, the snooty bitch needs ta be taken. Maybe I'll jest take her myself first then hand her over to the madam."

Rawls thought about that for a moment.

He noticed the madam talking to a man nearby and waved her over.

"Ya know anybody who kin git out a telegraph?"

"Hell no," Lena said. "Nobody leaves the Pass once they're in it. You go outside an' you get caught!"

"Yeah, that's what I figured," Rawls replied.

"How would you like a new girl for yer stable?" Danton blurted out.

Lena's mind worked fast. Here were two stupid, smalltime outlaws who had trapped themselves in Brimstone like dozens of others. They all had big ideas that didn't pan out and they always came to her for help.

"Who is that girl?" Lena growled. "Is she trouble?"

"She's nobody," Danton said.

"Don't you shit me, mister!" the madam hissed. "She don't look like she's a nobody."

"She the daughter of a rich rancher," Rawls said. "What does it matter who she is?"

"You two done broke the code! You dumb bastards!"

The big woman stomped off.

Rawls and Danton stared at each other.

"Why the hell is she a-chompin' at the bit?" Danton asked.

"We gotta git the hell outta here, you idiot!" Rawls said.

"We can't!" Danton said. "Unless ya want ta face the rope!"

"You sure fixed us up good, Kent!" Rawls chuckled.

Danton shrugged. All of a sudden he didn't feel so tough.

13.

They had Sherry Gadden's horse and a packhorse carrying supplies with them. At the end of a long day they camped under the overhang of a cliff, out of the wind. Old Tim built a fire and they ate jerky and hardtack and drank coffee. The coffee was strong and bitter.

"Christ," Jared complained. "This is strong enough to peel paint."

"Drink up," Tim chuckled. "It's good fer ya."

The old man opened a can of peaches and they shared it.

"How's it work in there?" Jared asked when they had finished eating.

Tim stroked his stubbly chin. "Well, they got rules in there, ya see, so we have ta go by the rules."

Jared laughed. "You're tellin' me a place full of robbers and cutthroats has rules?"

"Yep. Jest the same as we do."

Jared shrugged and looked out into the black night. He could hear the wind whispering in the pine trees nearby. A coyote howled out in the distance.

He finally spoke. "Where are you from, old man?"

"Texas, sonny boy," Tim replied. "Down near Amarillo."

"What'd you go to prison for?"

"Same as ever-body else, robbin' banks an' trains and such. They use ta call me the Canadian Kid 'cause I came from a place by the Canadian River, up in the panhandle."

Jared smiled. He wondered if the old man was pulling his leg. He didn't look like a gunfighter or an outlaw.

"When did you take up cooking for a living?"

"In prison. I was the cook's helper. When somebody up an' strangled him one day, I took his place."

"Well, you're a damn good one."

"Nobody's ever complained," Tim said with a smile. "They knows best not to."

The wind picked up and it started to get colder. They cut pine branches to sleep on.

It was a miserable night. They rose at dawn, built up the fire and stood close to it, chewing on warmed up jerky and drinking steaming coffee. An hour later they mounted up and rode on. Tim took the lead.

They passed small towns, crossed a railroad and rode across cattle country. Several times they saw farmers in the fields and cowboys moving their cows. Once they saw what looked like a posse of six men.

"Them is vigilantes or bounty hunters," Tim said. "We're close to Brimstone Pass."

The men rode up to them.

"Where ya headed?" the leader said.

"Brimstone Pass," Tim said.

"What fer?"

"Bix Rawls an' Kent Danton took Jim Gadden's girl in there."

The leader laughed. "Jest the two of you?"

"Yep," old Tim said.

"You must be crazy, then," the leader said. "You'll die in there. It'll take a whole lot more than the two of you."

A shorter, leaner and younger cowboy nudged his horse up alongside the leader. He addressed Tim.

"Did I hear ya say somebody took Sherry Gadden?"

"Yeah, why?" Tim asked. "You know her?"

"Hell, do I? Every rancher's son from here ta Belcher Springs knows Sherry Gadden."

"I hope ya mean thet well," old Tim growled.

"I do!" the cowboy said. "She's a lady if there ever was one, sir."

"Who the hell are you, old man?" the leader asked Tim. "A lawman?"

"A lawman? Hell, no," Tim replied. "I'm better than a lawman. I'm Gadden's chuck wagon ramrod."

A wave of laughter rippled through the cowboys. The leader almost doubled over. Finally he stopped to catch his breath.

"A cook, huh? Well, good luck, old-timer," he said. He looked at Jared. "An' who the hell are you, cowboy?"

"Jared. Clay Jared."

"Never heard a you."

"I have." A cowboy in the rear inched his horse up close. "I use ta work for the Triangle D, Colonel Denver's spread. Jared worked fer the Box R when the two went ta war. It was a blood bath on both sides. He was right in the middle of it."

Suddenly everyone spread out, leaving Jared and the cowboy facing one another, several feet apart.

"That's in the past," Jared said. "It's all over. Done with."

"My pard was kilt in thet war. Maybe you kilt him."

"Maybe I didn't," Jared said, dropping the reins of his horse. "I had some friends killed, too."

"Wal, it's stuck in my craw, Jared," the cowboy growled. "It looks like we're the last two a-standin'. Let's finish it."

"Are you sure? We don't have to. Let's just shake and forget the whole thing."

The others backed farther away out of the line of fire.

"I can't," the cowboy said.

"Alright. It's you're call."

"On the ground or in the saddle?" the cowboy asked.

"I'm in a hurry. In the saddle."

The cowboy drew.

A shot echoed in the frigid winter air but it wasn't from the cowboy's gun. Jared's Colt was out first. Smoke curled up from its barrel. His bullet hit the cowboy in the left shoulder, knocking him backward onto the hard ground, sending his gun flying.

Jared holstered his gun and dismounted. He walked over to where the cowboy sat holding his shoulder.

"Get the medicine box, Tim," he said.

The old man dismounted and got the medicine box from the packhorse. In a few moments Jared was attending to the cowboy's wound. When he finished he patted him on the back.

"Are we square now?"

The cowboy nodded. "Yeah. You winged me fair an' square, Jared. I guess ya coulda kilt me, but ya didn't. We're square."

"Christ," the leader said. "You're sure fast, Jared. Why don't ya join up with us?"

Jared chuckled. "Thanks for asking but I ride for Gadden's Diamond G right now."

"We'll go with ya and the old man to the Pass," the leader said. "We were headed that way when we met ya."

They hit the opening in the wall to Brimstone Pass late that afternoon. The leader of the vigilantes shook Jared's hand.

"We'll be hangin' around out here fer a few days. Don't tell anyone."

"I won't," Jared said. "Is there anyone special in there you're looking for?"

"Anybody with a bounty on his head will do," the leader chuckled.

Jared and Tim waved and rode into the opening of Brimstone Pass.

14.

The opening in Brimstone Pass led into a ravine that twisted and turned its way through high limestone cliffs that almost shut out the light. At the end of the passage they met two hunters with shotguns who each had a bag of small game slung over their shoulders.

"Howdy!" Tim said.

They gave Tim and Jared an intense glare.

"Howdy yerself," the tall one said. "What's yer game?"

"We're a-comin' in," was all Tim replied.

"Sanctuary?"

Tim nodded.

Suddenly one of the two men, the old one, squinted at Tim. He held his gaze a moment and then began to chuckle.

"Well, kiss my ass!" he said. He turned to the other man and said, "Hey, Al, this is the Canadian Kid! From around Ammy-rilly! We rode together in the old days."

Tim laughed. "I ain't the Canadian Kid no more, Dave. I'm jest Tim the cook now."

"Went clean, did ya?"

"Clean as a whistle, Dave."

"What the hell brings ya back ta tha Pass, Tim?"

"We think a couple of hombres brung a girl here."

"Yeah, last week," Al said. "Two big fellahs dressed like gunslingers."

"Well, they kidnapped thet girl from her pappy. We come ta git her back."

"Is they a reward fer her?"

"Nope. She's my boss's daughter."

"Well, good luck ta you, friend. Them two has got everybody a-pissin' in their boots," Dave said.

"Yeah," Al said. "They drilled Scarface Sully jest fer the fun of it. Fer no reason a-tall!"

"Any big names in here now?" Tim asked.

Dave rubbed his chin, thinking. "Let's see, Toothache Murphy, Bonehead Thompson, Horseface Tanner an' Slug Bannister, ta name a few."

"Never heard of 'em." Tim said.

"Al an' me, we mind our own business," Dave said. "We stay outta the way. Let them assholes kill each other."

"Who's yer pard?" Dave asked, looking at Jared.

"This is Kid Jared," Tim said with a straight face. "From around San Antone."

"Is he fast?"

"Tolerable so."

"Wal, tolerable won't git it done in tha Pass," Al cut in. "Tha graveyard is full of tolerable ones."

"Wal, we ain't lookin' fer no action, are we pard?" Tim grinned. Jared nodded in agreement. "We jest want the girl is all."

"Lotsa luck there, Tim," Dave said. "Ifn ya need a backup, jest let me and Al know."

"Thanks, Dave. Who's the mayor?" Tim asked.

"Les Notch," Al replied.

"How is he?"

"He's a decent fellow," Al said. "But he ain't got much backbone."

Tim and Dave talked for a while more, then he and Jared rode down to the settlement below. People stared and dogs barked at them as they rode up the muddy main street. Sometimes someone waved at Tim and he waved back. It was like a homecoming to the old man.

"Some of the old-timers are still here," he said. "They remember old Tim, I reckon." They passed the saloon and hotel porch. Several rough, grubby-looking men and women stood watching as they rode by. They smoked and drank. The women called out to Jared and waved for him to stop.

"Looks like a nice, friendly place," Jared said.

"Don't let it fool ya, sonny," old Tim chuckled. "It kin git real nasty in the blink of an eye."

They came to a small pine log building that had a sign above the door that read: Lester Notch, Mayor. After tying to the rail they went in.

Mayor Notch was sitting in a chair behind his desk. A pretty young girl half his age sat on his lap. He had just said something funny and she was giggling. When the mayor saw Tim and Jared he pushed her aside, stood up and straightened his clothes. She quickly left.

"Welcome to Brimstone, gentlemen," the mayor said, clearing his throat. "There will be a hundred-dollar residency fee each, if you please."

"We're not stayin', Mayor," Tim said. "We jest came ta git the girl."

The mayor sat down. "I wondered when somebody would show up about her."

"Where is she?" Jared asked.

"Who are you, sir?"

"I'm Clay Jared and I ride for the Diamond G. The girl is my boss's daughter. We're here to take her home."

"Well, good luck with that," Notch said. "Two others tried to take her from Rawls and Danton. They got a bullet in the head for their efforts."

"Where is she?" Tim asked.

"Over at the Yellow Dog Saloon."

Jared asked, "Where's Rawls and Danton?"

"They're there with her." The mayor shook his head. "You took a big chance comin' in here like this. I don't think you'll get out alive once they find out what you two are up to."

"Would ya like ta git rid of them two sidewinders, Mayor?" Tim asked.

"Sure I would."

"Then do as I tell ya and they'll be outta yer hair in no time."

The mayor laughed. "A few others tried it and died. You think you can get it done?"

"I sure kin," the old man said with a straight face. "Do ya know who I was once?"

"No. Who?"

"I was the Canadian Kid, thet's who. Maybe ya heard stories about me."

The mayor choked back a snicker. He cleared his throat again. "Sorry, I can't say that I have."

Jared cut in. "Rawls and Danton broke the code and you let them stay here. That makes you as guilty as they are."

"They lied," the mayor said. "They told me Danton and her were engaged!"

Tim ran around the desk and grabbed a fistful of the mayor's coat.

"Why the hell would anyone come here ta git hitched? Ya gotta be stupid as dirt ta swallow thet story, you dumb son of a bitch." He yanked the mayor out of his chair into a standing position. "I ought ta drill yer ass good."

Jared pulled his Colt and jammed the barrel against the mayor's big belly. "Maybe I'll do it for you, pard. Give me some room."

The mayor threw his arms up. "Wait a minute, men. Tell me what you want, please. I'll do anything you say!"

"We're goin' down ta the saloon," Tim said, "an yer gonna tell Rawls and Danton to come out."

"You're bracing them?"

"Thet's right," Tim growled.

"Christ! You're gonna get killed if you do that, old man."

"Thet's not yer worry, Mr. Mayor." Tim said and gave Notch a shove towards the door. "Let's go."

"Hell, it's your funeral," the mayor muttered as he went out the door. "Don't say I didn't warn you."

As they walked along the plank sidewalk to avoid the mud, Jared came alongside the mayor.

"You sound educated, Mayor. What were you?"

"An accountant."

"An embezzler?"

"Something like that, yes."

Jared chuckled. "You mean a lot like that."

The mayor shrugged and kept on walking. They finally came to the Yellow Dog Saloon.

"Make it quick," Jared said. "And no tricks."

As the mayor went in the saloon, the old man and Jared stepped out into the middle of the road.

"I hate this shitty place," Tim growled.

"Yeah," Jared said. "And it smells like rotten eggs."

"Thet's not the town," Tim corrected. "Thet's the sulfur bogs outside a town."

Suddenly the mayor came through the batwing doors of the saloon. Rawls and Danton were behind him. Danton had a gun in the mayor's back, using him for a shield. They stood looking down at the old man and the cowboy. Danton began to laugh.

"Well, well," Rawls sneered. "Whatta we got here?"

"I'm Tim Seely of the Diamond G. Mr. Gadden, my boss, sent me ta git the girl."

"Whatta ya do at the Diamond G, old man?" Rawls asked.

"I run the chuck wagon."

Danton laughed hard. "Christ! They sent the cook? Kin ya believe thet, Bix?"

"They must be hard up or in bad shape," Rawls sneered.

"Go back an' tell yer boss he kin have the bitch fer ten thousand," Danton said. "But I can't say how good a shape she'll be in." He chuckled.

"Who was the first one ta put a hand on her?" Tim asked.

"Me," Danton said, smiling.

"You?"

"That's right. Whatta ya gonna do about it, ya old fart?"

"I reckon I'll have ta brace ya, then."

Danton stepped away from Rawls and took up the stance.

"Draw, ya ol' piece of shit!" the outlaw cried out as he went for his gun.

Old Tim was way ahead of the outlaw.

He dropped down on his knees in the frozen street as Danton went for a head shot. His aim was high and missed the target. The old man's hand was a blur as he drew and shot upward. His bullet went through Danton's neck and out the top of his head. The big man's body jerked like crazy as he fired off another shot that went wild. He finally fell face first into the muddy street.

When Rawls saw what happened, he grabbed the mayor, hugged him close and tried to pull him back into the cover of the saloon. Jared drew, aimed carefully and took a shot. The Colt barked and the bullet nicked the mayor's left earlobe as it hit Rawls between the eyes.

The mayor grunted and ran back towards his office on the plank sidewalk, groaning. Rawls fell to his knees then onto his face on the saloon porch.

Jared turned to the old man. "You really were the Canadian Kid, weren't you? You old fart!"

"Didn't I say so?"

"Let's go!" Jared said.

"I'm with you, pard."

With guns drawn, they walked slowly into the saloon. Everyone inside froze and stared at them.

"We come fer the girl." Tim said. "Where is she?"

The bartender put his scattergun away as Lena slinked over to Jared. She looked him over and smiled.

"The girl ain't here no more, handsome," she said. "She jest lit out with Backstabber Conley and Tac Ordway. About a half hour ago."

"Son of bitch!" Tim groaned. "Which a way did they go?"

"They went out the back way. Most likely they're going through the sulfur bogs."

"Christ, they must be crazy ta go thet a way," the old man groaned.

"I sure feel sorry fer thet poor girl," someone said.

Tim and Jared left the saloon at a run and headed back up the street to get their horses.

15.

Backstabber's real name was Fern Conley. He was born in the suburbs of Chicago in the shadow of a steel mill that mostly made train rails. His father, who drank too much, worked there. As a young boy Fern went to a small school near the mill and its shadow passed over the school as the sun moved to the west. When that happened the classroom went dark and dreary.

One day, young Fern came home from school to see his father beating his mother with a hammer. He was in a drunken rage after being fired for showing up at work soused. When he was in that condition he blamed all his failures on Fern and his mother.

The young boy got a knife from the kitchen and stabbed his father in the back at least sixteen times. It was hard to tell exactly how many times but it was at least that many, according to the police.

Fern's mother died in the hospital, and the boy was sent to prison for fifteen years. He served every day of his sentence, and when he got out he went to work in the same steel mill his father had worked in. It was backbreaking work and Conley didn't like it at all. Not only was it hard, but it was boring and repetitious. Fern worked there for six months, then quit and went on the road.

After a couple of years of drifting from job to job, he hooked up with a troupe of traveling actors who took him on as a stagehand, repairing sets and so forth.

The troupe called itself The Traveling Theatre. They had come from the eastern seaboard but were now heading west. Their most popular play was called *The Perils of Little Nell*. In a year, Fern was acting and his name appeared on the playbill.

During this time Fern fell in love with the wife of the owner of the troupe who was also the director. They met secretly whenever they could, wherever they could, usually while her husband was dallying with one of the other female members of the group.

They were outside of Kansas City when Fern and the director's wife got caught in a compromising position. The woman's husband came at Fern and they fought. The man was bigger and stronger and soon had Fern by the throat, choking the life out of him. That's when the man's wife took a granite bust of Shakespeare and clobbered her husband over the head with it, crushing in the side of his skull.

They both stood there in shock for a moment. Fern took the bust from the woman's hands just as people came rushing into the tent. When they saw Fern holding the bloody object they pointed at him and screamed, "Murderer! Police!"

Fern ran for his life towards the stockyards and jumped onto an empty cattle train returning to western Kansas to reload. Among the crowd of misfits on the car was a man named Tac Ordway. He was Fern Conley's complete opposite: big, rough and uneducated. Ordway took to Conley and the two became close friends. The law was after Ordway for shooting a man in Abilene, and he was going to a place called Brimstone Pass to escape.

He painted a picture of easy days and fun nights in the Pass. As he described it, it was a place where the law never bothered anyone, beautiful women threw themselves at you and life was just one big party.

Fern Conley believed every word of it and went with Tac Ordway to the outlaw paradise called Brimstone Pass.

It didn't take long for Conley to find out that Brimstone Pass resembled Hades more than it resembled paradise. Since he was not a skilled gambler, he had to beg Lena, the owner of the Yellow Dog Saloon, for a job. When the place closed at two in the morning, Conley would come in with mop, broom and bucket to sweep and scrub the filth off the floor. He also had to clean the spittoons. It was a six-hour chore and for it he was allowed to sleep in a small room upstairs and eat in the kitchen.

Ordway did much better. He won at cards and was an accomplished pickpocket. He also waylaid drunks in the alleys of Brimstone. He always had money to spend and gave some to Conley. He rented a room near where Conley slept.

One day while drinking, Conley blurted out to Ordway how he had murdered his father. Others nearby heard the confession and quickly gave him the nickname of Backstabber Conley.

One day two men brought a beautiful young girl into the Yellow Dog Saloon, Fern Conley instantly fell in love with her. She never noticed him but he watched her closely. When the story went around that she had been stolen from her rich father, every outlaw in the Yellow Dog took notice of her.

A few made to take her away from Rawls and Danton but only ended up dead on the floor of the Yellow Dog or in the muddy street outside.

Fern Conley was among the many who had aspirations concerning the girl. He learned her name was Sherry Gadden.

"If we could get her out of here somehow, Tac, I bet her father would be most grateful," Conley said. "I'm thinking of a big reward." He was dying to get out of the Pass.

"Yeah, but there ain't no way of gettin' her away from those two gunnies. They're real fast on the draw."

"What if a chance came? Would you take it?"

"There ain't no way outta here without gettin' caught by the law. They're waitin' out front with a rope."

"There's a way out the back."

"The sulfur bogs?"

"Yes."

Tac Ordway considered that for a moment.

"Maybe we could. If she'd a-go wif us."

"Yes, that is the question, isn't it?"

"We'd need at least three horses," Ordway said.

"Yes." Conley saw that Ordway was hooked.

"One fer you, me an' her, with three saddlebags full of food. Can you shoot a gun?"

"Ah, no, I can't," Fern replied.

"That's alright. I'd do all the shootin', if it comes ta thet," Ordway added.

It took a few days but Ordway managed to get the horses and supplies and hide them in an old, abandoned shack behind the Yellow Dog Saloon. Then he and Conley waited.

Three days later the mayor came into the saloon and went up to the table where Rawls and Danton sat with the Gadden girl and two bar girls. Conley and Ordway sat at a table close enough to hear the conversation.

"What's up, Mayor?" Rawls asked.

"Ah, there's two cowboys outside demanding your attention."

"We're bein' braced?" Danton asked.

"I'm afraid so."

Danton chuckled. "Hell, why didn't ya jest come right out an' say it? We ain't gonna bite ya, Mayor."

The mayor giggled nervously.

Danton looked at Rawls. "Whatta you think, pard?"

"Who are they?" Rawls asked.

"Two cowboys who work for the girl's father," the mayor said. "One's a cowboy and the other is an old fart, a cook."

"A cowboy an' a cook?" Danton broke out laughing.

"Anybody else out there?" Rawls asked cautiously.

"Nope," the mayor said.

"You sure?" Danton asked. The mayor nodded.

Rawls and Danton stood up and checked their guns for full load. Rawls looked at the mayor.

"You go first, Mayor. We'll be right behind you."

The mayor looked scared. "I'll wait here, if you don't mind, Mr. Rawls?"

"But I do mind, Mayor," Rawls said coldly.

He gave the mayor a shove towards the batwing doors and followed him out onto the porch.

Conley saw his chance and took it. He ran over to Sherry Gadden.

"Miss Gadden, do you want to get out of here?"

"Yes, I do, sir!"

"Then please come with me."

"She ain't goin' no place," one of the bargirls said. She stood up and pulled a derringer out of her dress. Ordway hit her in the jaw. She collapsed on the floor.

The other girl held up her hands. "Hey, take the bitch. I don't care!"

Only a few drinkers seemed to notice as Conley, Ordway and Sherry Gadden snuck out through the back door of the Yellow Dog Saloon. The rest were at the windows looking out. They expected to see Bix Rawls and Kent Danton shoot down two cowboys in the street of Brimstone Pass.

It would be great fun to watch.

16.

Tac Ordway took the lead, with Sherry Gadden in the middle and Fern Conley behind. Ordway had only recently given Conley a few riding lessons, so he had trouble keeping up.

The trail wound through thickets of wild mulberry, bushes and vines. The ground here was warm enough to melt the snow. In some places it was soft and damp. Soon they could smell the suffocating odor of rotting eggs. As they went on, the ground got wetter and the horse's feet sank deeper into the mushy marshland.

An hour after forcing their way through dense vegetation, Conley cried out, "How much more of this?"

"Hell, I don't know," Ordway said, shouting back at him. "I never been here before. Just what I heard tell."

"Well, we'd better find dry ground before we sink out of sight," Sherry said. "The horses can't take much more of this."

They continued on and finally came to solid ground where a stand of wild sumac blocked their way. The ground was colder here and a thin layer of snow clung to the branches.

They skirted around the sumac and two hours later emerged into an open area just as it started to snow.

"Let's stop," Conley said. "Let the lady rest."

Nearby they found a small hollow beneath some tall bushes. The wind was picking up. They dismounted and got their bedrolls. Ordway scratched together enough kindling for a fire for coffee. They sat around eating jerky.

"Are you alright, Miss Gadden?" Conley asked.

"Yes, thanks," Sherry said. "Who are you, sir?"

"He's Backstabber Conley an' I'm Tac Ordway," the big outlaw said before Conley could answer.

"My real name is Fern, ma'am." Conley corrected.

"Where are you taking me, Mr. Conley?"

"He ain't a-takin' ya no place, ma'am," Ordway said. "I'm in charge here, an' ya kin deal wif me." Ordway took a sip of coffee. "Anyway, he's a-dyin'. He's got thet black lung disease."

"Is that true, Mr. Conley?"

"Alas, yes, Miss Gadden."

"He got it when they sent him ta prison fer stabbin' his own dad in the back," Ordway smirked. "Fifteen years in Storeyville busting rocks. Breathin' in the dust done him in."

"Is that true, Mr. Conley?"

Before he could answer Conley went into a coughing fit that wracked his body. He put a handkerchief to his mouth. It came away covered with black blood.

"I do have an ailment, Miss Gadden. Unfortunate, but true."

"Yep, he's a-dyin'," Ordway chuckled.

They sat silently by the fire for a few moments.

Suddenly Sherry noticed that Ordway was staring at her. His eyes seemed to dance in the firelight, almost glaring. He had an odd half-smile on his lips. It exposed his yellow, rotting teeth. His face looked almost demonic.

"You ever had a man?" he asked, smiling broadly.

The direct boldness of his question startled the girl. She looked over at Fern Conley.

"Now, Mr. Ordway," Conley said, turning to the big outlaw, "that is no way to talk to a lady, my good man."

Ordway gave his friend a cold look. "I'm a-talkin' ta her, Conley, not you, so butt out!" He added sarcastically, "An' I ain't yer good man."

"I thought we were friends, Mr. Ordway," Conley said.

Before Conley could respond, Sherry Gadden said, "If by men you mean male friends, Mr. Ordway, yes. I have had many suitors."

The big outlaw laughed.

"Well, it looks ta me like ya never had a real man take ya, little darlin'," Ordway sneered.

"I've never been taken, as you so crudely put it, by any man, sir, and I never will as long as I'm alive to prevent it!"

"Then I reckon I'll be the first!"

As Ordway reached out across the fire to grab Sherry Gadden's arm, Fern Conley swung at him, catching him in the side of his jaw and stopping him in his tracks. The outlaw grunted and felt the side of his jaw where he had been struck. Without warning he pulled his gun and shot Fern Conley in the chest.

Sherry screamed and jumped up. The outlaw holstered his gun and leaped over the fire at her.

The girl staggered backward, striking out to ward off his attack. In a moment he was on her and had her pinned to the ground in the snow. She screamed again and again. Ordway slapped her hard across the mouth. She spit blood into his eyes and brought her knee up into his groin, forcing him to groan in pain and fall back into the fire.

Ordway rolled clear of the flames but his coat was on fire. He danced around trying to slap it out, jumping up and down. Finally, he was able to get the coat off and toss it aside.

He let out a yell of rage and started to come at her again, then realized his holster was empty. He was looking down the barrel of his own gun. He stopped to glare over at her like a wounded animal.

"You bitch! Yer dead!" Ordway leaped at her.

Sherry Gadden fanned off three shots. One took Ordway in the belly, one in the heart and one hit him square between the eyes.

Dropping the gun, Sherry went over to where Fern Conley lay in the snow. She knelt next to him as he looked up at her with a smile. Blood bubbled from the corner of his mouth. Sherry took his handkerchief and dabbed at it.

"Thank you," Conley said. He had a peaceful look on his face. He smiled strangely as if seeing a vision. "I used to act on the stage," he muttered under his breath. Sherry smiled down at him and nodded.

"Were you good?"

"Oh, yes. Very good." He looked past her. "To be or not to be, that's is the question…"

The light went out of Conley's eyes. He relaxed in Sherry's arms and she knew he was dead.

She started to cry.

17.

The fire was almost out when Tim and Jared rode up to the camp. Sherry Gadden was still holding Fern Conley's cold body in her arms, rocking him like a baby. Her eyes stared off into the distance and she didn't seem to see them.

"Christ!" Tim said.

They dismounted. Jared walked over to Ordway's body.

"Somebody ventilated this one real good."

Tim went over to Sherry Gadden, leaned down and put a hand on her shoulder.

"Miss Gadden!" She didn't respond.

Jared came over and stared down at her. He knelt next to her and turned her face toward his. She didn't seem to see him. Jared gently slapped her twice. She suddenly shook her head and looked at him as if coming out of a dream.

"What? Is that you, Jared?"

"It's me and Tim. We're taking you home."

She shook her head to clear it.

Tim took hold of Conley's body and shifted it to one side as Jared helped Sherry to stand up. She clung to him for support.

"Are you real, cowboy?" Sherry asked, looking into his eyes.

"Yes."

"Who's this fellah, Miss Sherry?" Tim asked, nodding at Conley.

"He's Mr. Conley, a very nice man." Sherry looked down at the body and began to sob.

"We can't stay here," Jared said. "We'll have to follow the tracks back before the snow covers them."

"I'm sorry but I'm just too tired," Sherry sighed. "I can't."

"Don't worry about them tracks," Tim said. "We'll camp here. I'll stoke up the fire and make some coffee."

While Tim went to work, Jared moved the bodies over into a patch of brush out of eyesight. After that he got all the extra blankets and saddles from the horses and made three beds. He tied the horse's reins to some saplings where winter grass grew.

While Sherry lay down under two blankets, Jared and Tim gathered up enough dead branches to last throughout the night. They heated up some rocks and put them under Sherry's blanket by her feet. She soon fell asleep.

"I'll take the first watch," Tim said. He took out his pocket watch. "From now 'til three. Then you wake us up at dawn."

Jared nodded and crawled under the blankets.

It seemed as if he had just fallen asleep when Tim woke him up.

"There's fresh coffee on," he whispered and got in bed. In a few minutes he was snoring.

An hour before dawn Sherry woke up. She draped a blanket around her shoulders, walked over to Jared and put her head on his shoulder.

"You came for me. Why?"

"You know why."

She looked up at him. "Kiss me, if you want to."

"Alright."

He kissed her and held her close until dawn.

They had a quick breakfast, broke up camp and tied the extra horses in a train. As they were ready to go, Sherry hesitated.

"Couldn't we take Mr. Conley with us?"

"Sure, I guess," Tim said.

Tim and Jared tied Conley's body across the saddle of his horse and they started back to Brimstone Pass. The sky was dull and overcast. It started to snow again.

"I'll take the lead," Tim said.

Jared nodded. He looked at Sherry. "You alright?"

"Yes. Let's go."

It was late afternoon when they came through the sulfur bogs into the back entrance to Brimstone. Someone saw them coming and ran to tell the mayor.

They took Conley's body to the undertaker's place and offered the packhorse along with Ordway's gun and holster as payment. They kept Ordway's horse and the one Conley rode.

Once that was settled they tied up at the rail in front of the beanery, went in and ordered a steak smothered in onions with a side of pole beans and apple pie. After that they each had a bottle of the locally brewed beer called Bog Juice. The owner said she made it herself from yeast, honey and turnips.

"Not bad," Tim chuckled and had another bottle.

After eating, they sat and relaxed, feeling the calming effect of a good meal. Tim rolled a cigarette.

"We'll start out in the mornin'," he said.

"Will they try to stop us?" Sherry worried.

"Not as I kin see," the old man said. "I'd think they'd be glad ta see you go. You been nothin' but a pain in the ass, Miss Sherry," Tim chuckled.

Just then a little boy came into the beanery. He walked over to their table.

"Which of you is called Jared?"

"That would be me. Why?"

"Slug Bannister says ta come outside an' meet yer maker."

The little boy ran off.

Jared sighed. He pushed his chair back and checked his Colt.

"Don't go out there, Clay," Sherry pleaded.

"We're trapped," Jared said. "Even if we go out the back, it wouldn't do any good. There's no place to run."

"Let me go, sonny," Tim said.

Jared reached over and patted Tim's shoulder.

"No, you have another bottle of Bog Juice and keep an eye on Miss Gadden. I'll be right back."

Jared got up, laid several double eagles on the table and walked out into the street.

Slug Bannister was standing in the middle of the road, waiting as the snow fell. He was a tall, skinny man dressed in the fancy black clothes of a gunslinger. His wide-brimmed hat covered most of his face. Bannister's eye blazed with a fierce fire.

"Whatta you want with me, Bannister?" Jared asked.

"I want the girl, not you," the gunslinger said. "But I guess I gotta put you down ta git her and the ransom, right?"

Jared chuckled. "There isn't any ransom, you asshole. Rawls and Danton found that out."

"You gonna argue with me or shoot?"

"Draw!" Jared heard himself say.

Bannister's hand swung upward for his gun. It had just cleared the holster by an inch when he saw Jared's hand move so fast it became a blur. The gunman felt a sharp pain in his chest then heard the roar of Jared's Colt.

He tried to get his gun up to fire but his arm felt like it was made of lead, too heavy to move. A second bullet hit him in the heart and he was slammed backward on the road.

Tim came out of the beanery and stood beside Jared. He had his gun out and was looking around.

"Nice shootin', sonny," Tim said. "But a mite slow on the draw. I'd of took him a lot faster."

"Sure you would," Jared said.

Sherry came out and looked up the road at the body of Slug Bannister.

Suddenly the mayor was hurrying towards them on the plank sidewalk. He stopped to glance at Bannister's body and then continued up to them.

"You two owe the town ten double eagles," the mayor said.

"What fer?" Tim asked.

"For the burying of Rawls, Danton and now Bannister."

"You can have their horses and rigs," Jared said. "That should cover it."

The mayor didn't look too happy about that.

"Then give me three and be done with it."

Jared nodded and handed the mayor three double eagles.

"And if I were you, I would leave as soon as possible. Bannister has some very dangerous friends. They'll be coming after you, I expect. And real soon."

A crowd had gathered. Tim looked around and saw his old friend Dave. Al was with him. They still had their shotguns.

"Hi, Dave," Tim said.

"Ya need some help, ol' pard?" Dave asked.

"How about an escort out the front door, Dave?" Tim asked. "You an' Al kin have those two extra horses and saddles we was given by accident."

"Sure thing," Dave replied. "C'mon, Al. We finally got us a mount. No more walkin', pard!"

They all mounted up. Tim nodded at the mayor.

"Don't come back, old man," the mayor said. "Please don't come back."

"Kiss my bony ass, Mayor," Tim said.

They rode up the road to the incline leading out of the pass. They stopped to look back down at the settlement. The tents and cabins were covered with cotton. Dark smoke curled slowly heavenward from chimneys. They could barely make out the mayor's place and the Yellow Dog Saloon.

"Be seein' ya, Tim," Dave said.

"No ya won't, Dave," Tim chuckled.

The old man spit on the ground and nudged his horse up towards the outlet of the pass. Jared and Sherry followed.

As they rode through to the outside they saw a campfire not far away. It was the vigilantes. Several armed men came over to meet them. The leader recognized them from before.

"Are you Miss Gadden?" he asked, saluting.

"Yes."

"Welcome to the outside world, ma'am," he said. "Are you alright?"

"Yes, I'm fine. I'm going home now."

"God bless you, ma'am." The leader said.

"How far is the nearest place we can stay overnight?" Jared asked.

"About twenty miles on the old coach road. Hatton Flats. Mention the name of Frank Cahill. That's me."

"We'll be sure to do that, Mr. Cahill," Sherry said. "Thank you."

One of the cowboys asked, "Was there an outlaw in there by the name of Slug Bannister?"

"Yeah," Tim said. "Why?"

"He kilt my pappy. I'm a-waitin' fer him ta try an' sneak out."

"Well, you kin fergit about him. Jared here put a couple a lead pills in his belly."

They rode off for Hatton Flats.

18.

Three days later they rode into the front yard of the Diamond G. It was late afternoon and everyone came out to meet them. Jared, Tim and Sherry wearily dismounted. Sherry rushed into the arms of her father. He was almost crying. He clutched her close and stared over at Jared and Tim, nodding his gratitude.

Jared and the old man went down to the bunkhouse. Ramrod Phil Newly broke out a bottle of whiskey and they all toasted to the return of Sherry Gadden.

"Tell us about it," the carpenter, Ted Curtis, said.

"Tell ya 'bout it?" old Tim said. "Wal, I'll tell ya 'bout it! We left thet place in shambles, we did. Heck, we braced ever' one of them varmints. Left dead bodies all over the place."

"Oh-oh! Git the shovel, fellahs," Newly said. "The cow shit is gonna git pretty high in here any minute now!"

"What happened ta Rawls an' Danton, them bastards what killed Curt?"

Old Tim sniffed and wiped his nose on his coat sleeve.

"What happened ta them two, ya ask? We'll I'll tell ya what happened! Jared an' me, we braced them two sidewinders right on the porch of the Yeller Dog Saloon and shot 'em both ta ribbons!"

"You don't say!" someone said.

"Yep, I do say, an' it's the truth. Jest ask Jared."

Jared had just walked out of the bunkhouse moments earlier. He stood in the yard under the lean-to and rolled a cigarette while looking up at the house. He noticed the lamps were lit.

When he finished smoking the cigarette he walked over behind the house to a little plot of land with a low picket fence around it. There were a dozen headstones there, a history of the Gadden family. He found Curt's headstone and looked down at it for a while then went back to the horses.

In the excitement of the moment everyone had forgotten about them. He took up their reins and led the horses down to the barn. After un-cinching them and tossing the saddles, saddlebags, bridles and bedrolls over the stall fences, he fed them a bag of oats. After that he led them out to the water trough and let them drink, then put them in the corral. They seemed happy to be back with their friends. He stood there in the afterglow of evening looking up at the house.

The next day, late in the afternoon, he asked Phil Newly to send him out to the north line shack, the farthest point on the Diamond G.

"I can't," Newly said. He looked solemn. "The boss's orders."

They were down by the barn.

"I see," Jared said. "When is it coming?"

"That's up to you, Jared. You know what you have to do."

The cowboy nodded.

"Hell, I might just as well get it over. Get my pay, won't you?"

"Now?"

"Sure. Why hang on? It's over, isn't it?"

Newly nodded.

"I'm sorry. Yer the best cowpoke I ever had, Jared. If I had a say, you'd have a job fer as long as ya wanted."

"Thanks. That means a lot to me, Phil."

The ramrod sighed and looked away.

"I'll go draw yer wages, Jared."

Jared nodded. Newly walked up to the house and knocked.

Jared watched him go in. He could hear voices in the house. Sherry was angry. Finely the ramrod came back with Jared's money.

"Don't tell Tim until after I'm gone," Jared said.

"Alright. Sure."

They shook hands. Phil Newly stood for a moment looking at Jared. Finally, he nodded, turned and walked over to the bunkhouse. He stopped to nod again, then went in.

Jared got his horse from the corral and took it into the barn out of the snow. He put the saddle on and tied the saddlebag and bedroll to it. It was snowing hard out in the yard.

Sherry Gadden came running in without a coat, shaking the snow from her hair. She came up close to Jared.

"The bastard! After all you've done for him!"

"It's alright," Jared said, putting the hackamore in place.

She watched him working the saddle straps.

"It's my fault. I should never have gone out to the line shack."

"I'm glad you did. It was worth it."

Sherry turned her back to him to hide her eyes.

"He plans to marry me off to the son of Ben Dunham of the Box D."

"Big spread?"

"Yes."

"Smart move on your dad's part."

She spun around and faced him, grabbing his coat.

"Damn you!" She was crying. "Kiss me."

"No. Leave me alone." Jared's voice cracked.

"I'll never leave you alone as long as you're here, married or not!"

She kissed him. He took her in his arms and held her for a while.

"You'll forget all about me."

"No, I won't. I'll never forget you."

He gently pushed her away, tightened the cinch and swung up into the saddle. She grabbed the horse's head, and kissed it. She wiped the tears from her eyes.

"Where are you going, cowboy?"

"I don't know. West, maybe. Whichever way the wind blows, I guess."

"Good-luck. And stay away from those painted ladies."

"Sure."

Jared bent over in the saddle and touched her cheek with his hand. She grabbed it and held on until he pulled away.

Sherry Gadden watched Clay Jared as he slowly rode out into the yard, heading for the south road trail.

The snow began to fall harder. In a little while she couldn't see him anymore. Slowly, she walked back to the ranch house.

The End.

About the Author

As a young boy growing up in the city, R. Annan never passed up a chance to see a Western movie. His heroes were Buck Jones, Johnny Mack Brown, Wild Bill Elliot and John Wayne, to name a few. As an adult, he often wondered where his love of Westerns came from. Perhaps it has something to do with his grandfather, John L. Annan, who was a cowboy from Helena, Montana, in days of old.

A Note from the Author

Thank you for reading my book. If you enjoyed it, would you please consider rating and reviewing it? I'd enjoy your feedback.

Look for other books to appear soon. Thank you!